Stone Age Adventures

Little Nut's Big Journey

By Vivian French
Illustrated by Cate James

W
FRANKLIN WATTS
LONDON • SYDNEY

The Stone Age Family

Chapter One

The evenings were getting dark and the days were getting shorter. Old Boulder looked up at the sky. "Snow soon," he said. "Tomorrow we move." Little Nut stared at him. "Move?"

Pim put her arm round him. "Don't you remember? It's nearly winter. We always move to the cave for winter." Little Nut frowned. "Little Nut stay. Little Nut not like cave!"

Pod made a face at his little brother.

"Yes, you do, silly. It's warm and cosy in the cave. It gets freezing here in the hut!"

"We'll meet Uncle and Auntie and the cousins," Pim said. "And we'll all snuggle up together and Auntie will tell us stories."

Mama Boulder was piling the pots into a heap. "We'll take these," she said. "Pim, tomorrow you collect the furs. We'll have to start early. We travel all day."

"Will we go over the river bridge?" Pim asked. "That's scary!" Pod put his hands on his hips. "No, it's not! It's easy peasy!"

"Peasy!" agreed Little Nut.

"BED!" said Dada Boulder, picking up Little Nut and dropping him on his bed. "Remember – we start early tomorrow!"

Chapter Two

Little Nut was the first to jump out of bed.

"Up!" he shouted, and he pulled the furs away from Pim and Pod. "Go scary river! Go NOW!"

Pod yawned. "It's dark. It's still night-time!"

Gramma peered out of the doorway. “No ... the sun will be here soon.”

“I’m going to pack the furs,” Pim told her. “Come on, Pod. You can help.”

“I’m going to collect the fishing rods,”

Pod said. “That’s a grown-up job.”

“Be careful,” Gramma warned.

“Mind the hooks!”

It took another hour to pack up the pots and furs and precious flints, but at last they were ready. Everyone had something to carry, even Little Nut.

"Good," said Dada Boulder. "It's still early! Off we go!" Pim patted the side of the hut they were leaving. "Goodbye, summer house. We'll see you in the spring," she said.

They walked in single file. Remember – watch and listen!" Old Boulder warned. "Bears are sleepy, but wolves are hungry!"

“I’m not afraid of wolves,” Pod boasted. “I’m not afraid of anything!”

“Not afraid!” Little Nut echoed, but Old Boulder shook his head. “Best to be a little frightened. Fear keeps ears sharp!”

Pim was squinting ahead of her. “Do we go through the forest?” “Don’t you remember?” Pod asked. “Through the forest, then down to the river and over the bridge.”

Chapter Three

It was late in the afternoon by the time they reached the river. Old Boulder was carrying Little Nut, and everyone was tired.

“There’s the bridge!” Pod said.

The river ran between high rocky cliffs. The bridge was an old tree trunk that had fallen across the narrow gap. The water swirled and bubbled far below.

Pim looked at the tree trunk, her heart beating fast. There was a rope made of twisted reeds, but it swayed and swung, and didn't look safe.

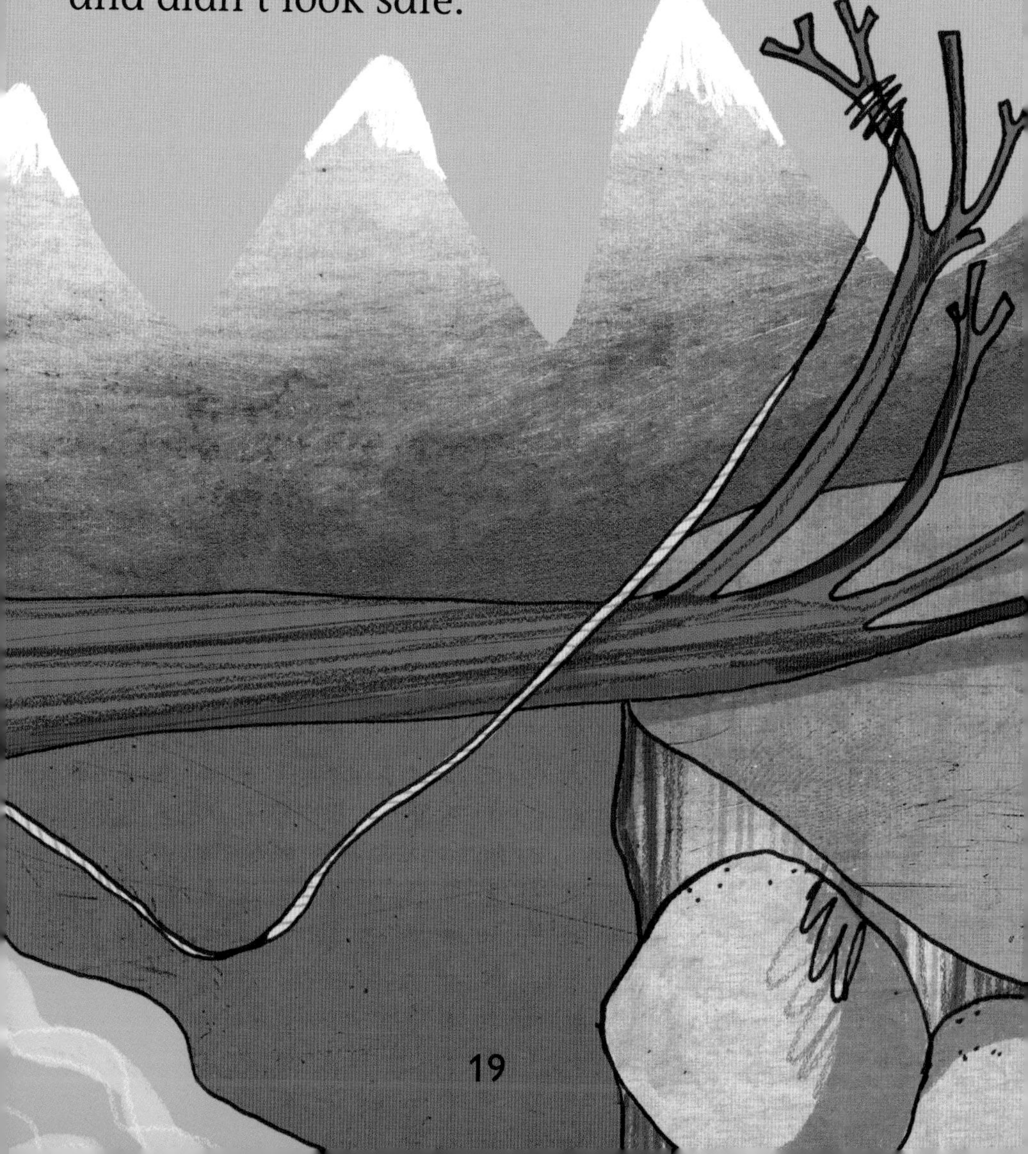

"Can I go first?" Pod asked. Dad inspected the tree, then tugged at the rope. "Strong enough. You can go." Pod grinned, and two minutes later he was on the other side. "Easy peasy!" he shouted.

Mama Boulder went next, slowly and carefully. Dad carried Little Nut across, and put him down by the rocks on the other side. He came back for a load of pots and furs, and over he went again.

Pim took a deep breath. It was her turn next. “Don’t look down,” Gramma told her. “Look at Dada!” Clutching the rope and looking straight ahead, Pim balanced her way over the tree trunk. “Phew!” she said. “I’ve done it!”

Chapter Four

Gramma went last. She was almost at the other side when she slipped ..."AHHHH!" she yelled. "HELP!" and she slithered off the tree. A rock broke her fall, and she grabbed it and hung on tightly.

"The rope! Throw her the rope!" Old Boulder shouted. Pod ran to try to untie the end, but he couldn't reach. The rope was tied too high. "I'll lift you up!" Old Boulder said and swung Pod onto his shoulders. Pod heaved and tugged at the knot, but it wouldn't undo.

"Pim! Try the other end!" Mama Boulder was crouching, trying to reach Gramma's hand. Pim gulped. The other end was back over the bridge ... could she do it?

Pim swung round. "Here goes!" Staring straight ahead, she walked firmly across the tree trunk. The knots were easy to untie. As soon as Pim had undone the rope, Pod jumped down from his tree and reeled it in to his side of the river.

Mama Boulder lowered the rope down to Gramma, and the old woman seized it. A moment later Old Boulder heaved her up to safety. "Hurrah!" shouted Pod and Little Nut.

On the other side of the river, Pim cheered too. "Hurrah!"

Chapter Five

"Well done, Pim!" Mama Boulder clapped. Old Boulder looked worried. "But now there's no rope to help Pim come back!"

"Me help Pim," said a small voice. Before anyone could stop him, Little Nut had picked up the end of the rope. The next minute he was half running, half skipping his way over the tree trunk.

Pim held her breath while she watched – and when her little brother reached her, she gave him a huge hug. "You're a hero, Little Nut!" she told him. Little Nut's eyes were sparkling as he helped Pim tie the rope firmly to a tree. Together they crossed the bridge for the final time.

"Little Nut a hero!" he said. Old Boulder nodded. "A real hero," he said, and he swung Little Nut onto his shoulders. "And now, let's be on our way!"

The sun was just setting as they reached the cave. Auntie, Uncle and the cousins were waiting, and the fire was burning brightly. "Come and sit," Uncle said. "Sit, and tell us a story while the meat is roasting." Dada smiled. "I have a story to tell," he said. "A story of three brave and clever children! Pod, Pim and Little Nut!"

Life in the Stone Age

The Stone Age began around 2.6 million years ago. It is called the Stone Age as people used tools and weapons made of stone. Families often had to relocate depending on the seasons. In winter, ice and snow meant finding cosy caves to live in until it got warm. Then they could camp in less sheltered places. There was no such thing as a fixed home.

Franklin Watts
First published in Great Britain in 2015 by
The Watts Publishing Group

Series Editor: Melanie Palmer
Series Advisor: Catherine Glavina
Series Designers: Peter Scoulding and Cathryn Gilbert

ISBN 978 1 4451 4273 9 (hbk)
ISBN 978 1 4451 4276 0 (pbk)
ISBN 978 1 4451 4275 3 (library ebook)

Printed in China

MIX
Paper from responsible sources
FSC® C104740

Franklin Watts
An imprint of
Hachette Children's Group
Part of The Watts Publishing Group
Carmelite House
50 Victoria Embankment
London EC4Y 0DZ

An Hachette UK Company
www.hachette.co.uk

www.franklinwatts.co.uk